BROWNIE&PEARL
Go for a Spin

by CYNTHIA RYLANT ✿ pictures by BRIAN BIGGS

Beach Lane Books
New York London Toronto Sydney New Delhi

Look who's coming!
It's Brownie and Pearl.

Brownie has a car.
It has a seat for Pearl.

They are going for a spin.

Brownie drives to the mailbox.
Pearl gets the mail.

Pearl gets **all** the mail!

Next they deliver the mail.

"Going for a spin?"
someone asks.

YES!

Brownie drives back home.

She parks her car.
Pearl doesn't want to get out.

Pearl won't get out.
Pearl likes the car.

Brownie has an idea.
She runs inside.

Soon she is back.
She has treats.

Pearl is so happy.

She **loves** takeout!

For Mike and Polly Ann
—B. B.

BEACH LANE BOOKS
An imprint of Simon & Schuster Children's Publishing Division
1230 Avenue of the Americas, New York, New York 10020

For information about special discounts for bulk purchases, please contact Simon & Schuster Special Sales
at 1-866-506-1949 or business@simonandschuster.com.
The Simon & Schuster Speakers Bureau can bring authors to your live event. For more information or to book an event,
contact the Simon & Schuster Speakers Bureau at 1-866-248-3049 or visit our website at www.simonspeakers.com.
Book design by Sonia Chaghatzbanian
The text for this book is set in Berliner Grotesk.
The illustrations for this book are rendered digitally.
Manufactured in China
1211 SCP
First Edition
2 4 6 8 10 9 7 5 3 1
Library of Congress Cataloging-in-Publication Data
Rylant, Cynthia.
Brownie & Pearl go for a spin / by Cynthia Rylant ; pictures by Brian Biggs.—1st ed.
p. cm.
Summary: When Brownie and her cat go for a spin in her car, neither one is ready for it to end.
ISBN 978-1-4169-8633-1 (hardcover)
ISBN 978-1-4424-3911-5 (eBook)
[1. Automobiles—Fiction. 2. Cats—Fiction.] I. Biggs, Brian, ill. II. Title. III. Title: Brownie and Pearl go for a spin.
PZ7.R982Bre 2012
[E]—dc22
2010018320